D0470851

A Name On the Quilt

A Name On

the Quilt

A STORY OF REMEMBRANCE

by JEANNINE ATKINS

illustrated with pictures by TAD HILLS

and photographs of panels from the AIDS Memorial Quilt

WITHDRAWN

UNIVERSITY OF NV LAS VEGAS
CURRICULUM MATERIALS LIBRARY
101 EDUCATION BLDG
LAS VEGAS, NV 89154

ATHENEUM BOOKS FOR YOUNG READERS

Atheneum Books for Young Readers
An imprint of Simon & Schuster Children's Publishing Division
1230 Avenue of the Americas
New York, New York 10020

Text copyright © 1999 by Jeannine Atkins
Illustrations copyright © 1999 by Frederic Hills
Photographs copyright © 1999 by The NAMES Project Foundation
All rights reserved including the right of reproduction in whole or in part in any form.

The text of this book is set in Berkeley.
The illustrations are rendered in colored pencil and watercolor, acrylic, and oil paints.

First Edition
Printed in Hong Kong
10 9 8 7 6 5 4 3 2 1

Library of Congress Cataloging-in-Publication Data
Atkins, Jeannine, 1953–
A name on the quilt : a story of remembrance / by Jeannine Atkins ; illustrated with pictures by
Tad Hills and photographs of panels from the AIDS memorial quilt.—1st ed.
Summary: A family reminisces while gathered together to make a panel for the AIDS Memorial
Quilt in memory of a beloved uncle.
ISBN 0-689-81592-1 (hc)
[1. NAMES Project AIDS Memorial Quilt—Fiction. 2. AIDS (Disease)—Fiction. 3. Grief—Fiction.
4. Uncles—Fiction.] I. Hills, Tad. II. Title.
PZ7.A8634Nam   1999
[Fic]—dc21   97-42303

FIRST
EDITION

For Karen Lederer,
Brian Sabel, and
Rosa Lederer-Sabel
—J. A.

For Elinor
—T. H.

× × × × × × × × × × × ×

Lauren swung open the door to let in some of Uncle Ron's old friends. The last time Michael, Jan, and Henry had been at Lauren's house, they'd stamped snow off their boots. The living room had been filled with boxes of tissues and plates of bagels that tasted stale. Several months had passed since Uncle Ron had died. Now, as Lauren opened the door again for Grandma, the breeze was almost warm on her cheeks.

Everyone gathered in the living room where Mom and Dad were flapping open pieces of cloth. The fabric rustled, like the sound of opening presents. An ironing board stood where Lauren's dog usually napped.

✕ ✕ ✕ ✕ ✕ ✕ ✕ ✕ ✕ ✕ ✕ ✕ ✕ ✕ ✕ ✕ ✕

"What are we going to do with all of these things?" Lauren's younger brother, Bobby, asked.

Lauren sighed. All week, while the family tried to get ready for today, Bobby did nothing but ask questions. She didn't think he would ever understand how important this was.

But Lauren's dad smiled patiently and said, "We're going to make the quilt panel for Uncle Ron now."

"I'll get the brownies," Lauren said, heading for the kitchen. As she picked up the plate, she remembered Uncle Ron and Michael's refrigerator, which was covered with her drawings. Their house was the only place where she'd always been given snacks in china bowls and juice in glasses that could break. All week, Lauren had been surprised by memories like these.

Lauren set the brownies on a table. The living room was starting to hum with activity. Pins and shiny sequins clinked as Jan poured them into cups. Henry and Michael rummaged through bags of Uncle Ron's old clothes they had brought from Michael's apartment. Lauren's cat scrambled after ribbons and spools.

Bobby ran over and jumped into Grandma's arms. "Where's Grandpa?" he asked. Grandpa hadn't come after Uncle Ron's memorial service either.

"Grandpa says he doesn't know how to sew," Grandma said.

Dad spread an old blanket, about the size of a man with his arms a little open, on the rug. Everyone took turns picking letters from Uncle Ron's whole name, Ronald Paul Nelson, to sew on the quilt. Lauren chose some green cloth because it reminded her of Uncle Ron's eyes and his garden. She traced an N onto her fabric, then carefully cut, ironed, and pinned the letter on the blanket. She tried to keep her stitches small, since Dad said those were the strongest.

Soon, they each had a section of the blanket and were busy at work.

"Lauren, remember when you were six, and Uncle Ron took you to the lake every Saturday?" Dad asked, sewing an *O* printed with fish.

"Yeah, we went even when it rained." Lauren smiled as she thought of Uncle Ron standing in the water, pretending to shiver madly while she got up the courage to dive for the first time. When she finally did, he whooped and spun her in a circle. Water splashed everywhere.

"Ron sure did love the water. If we passed a lake, he wanted to swim, even in October," Michael said, bending over the *R* he'd cut from Ron's plaid hiking shirt. "And in the winter, he couldn't wait for the pond to freeze up for ice skating."

Bobby ran around and draped ribbons over Mom. She tied a square of fabric around his neck like a cape. Then he swooped onto Lauren.

"Stop it! You're making me wiggle." Lauren pushed Bobby away.

"But I want to help!" Bobby said.

"You're too little," Lauren said.

"Here, Bobby," Dad said, handing him a marker to color in the P and L. "You can work on these."

"Don't let him scribble!" Lauren said. "This quilt has to look good."

"Don't worry so much, Lauren," Dad said gently. "He'll do just fine."

As she sewed, Lauren banged elbows with her mother and with Michael. Her toes grazed Grandma's knees. Lauren's stitches didn't always go where she aimed them, the way a tossed ball didn't always land where she meant it to.

"You know, Lauren, when Ron got too sick to leave the house, he still asked if the ice on the pond was thick enough for skating." Michael's voice was slow and quiet, more like Lauren's than Uncle Ron's. He knotted the end of his thread, then picked up a letter Mom had cut and sat down next to Lauren. "Ron remembered the way you two used to hold hands and scream as you whipped across the pond."

Lauren thought about the day that she and Uncle Ron had broken through some thin ice at the edge of the pond. Uncle Ron had pulled her out, yanked off her skates and socks, covered her cold feet with his mittens, and carried her partway home.

Lauren's thread slipped out of her needle. Her eyes watered as she thought of the feel and smell of Uncle Ron's wool jacket.

"It gets easier," Michael whispered, threading her needle.

Lauren and Michael went back to work. Conversation rose and fell as Uncle Ron's name took shape on the quilt.

Then Bobby crawled underneath it.

"Mom, Bobby is going to wreck this," Lauren complained. "He doesn't know we're doing something important."

Mom tugged Bobby out. "Lauren, you know he's too little to sit still. Besides, he didn't do any harm."

"Isn't it time for him to go to bed?" Lauren asked.

"No!" Bobby ran from the room.

Lauren sighed with relief. She changed places with Jan so she could sew on one of the last letters.

But in a minute, Bobby's bedroom door slammed. He came back with a pair of red socks in his hands. He looked small and alone in the doorway. "Ron gave these to me," Bobby said proudly.

"Do you remember playing catch with them when Uncle Ron was sick in bed?" Lauren asked, a little surprised.

"Yes," Bobby said. He held the socks carefully, like something that could break.

Lauren gave her brother a long look. *Of course he remembers,* she thought. *He remembers and misses Uncle Ron as much as I do.* "Do you want to sew the socks on the quilt?" she asked him.

Bobby's eyes were large and serious as he nodded.

"You know you won't have them to play with anymore," Lauren said.

"I know," Bobby said.

"Wait," Michael said. "There's a bunch more in one of these bags that we can use."

Bobby scooped out an armful of socks from a bag. Michael and Mom arranged them around Ron's name. Soon, everyone was telling new stories about Uncle Ron as they stitched on the socks that he had worn while skating, dancing, and climbing mountains.

Finally Lauren set down her needle. Scissors clicked as Michael cut some threads. Then, taking one end of the panel and giving the other end to Grandma, they held it up. Lauren gazed at what they had sewn together. Uncle Ron's bold socks seemed to dance around the edges. Even the letters that Bobby had colored looked perfect.

"Grandpa should have come. He should have seen this," Grandma said. She put her head on Dad's shoulder for a minute, then turned away. "I'd better find my coat. It's getting late."

Jan and Henry carried empty cups to the kitchen. The living room got quiet. Lauren thought about how Uncle Ron was always the last to leave. Mom would pour Lauren a cup of water and Dad would get out the Scrabble board, while Uncle Ron turned on the radio. He always said, "Let's have just one dance before Lauren has to go to bed."

"Uncle Ron loved to dance, didn't he, Mommy?" Lauren let her voice fill the room.

"He loved you, Lauren," Mom said.

For a minute the room was still. Then Michael said, "Ron wanted us to remember and make a quilt. But he wanted us to dance, too."

Dad turned on the radio. Everyone started dancing. Waving their arms, kicking their feet, it almost seemed as if Uncle Ron were with them. He would have laughed with Grandma, who looked silly and great dancing in her coat. He would have twirled Lauren and tossed Bobby in the air.

When the song was over, Lauren wrapped herself in the soft quilt panel. Coming or going, Uncle Ron had always hugged her so hard that her feet had left the ground. Now she hugged herself. Soon all the colors Uncle Ron had loved would clash and blend with others on the quilt that is as wide as a lake and as brilliant as the sky. Soon everyone would know his name.

Since 1987, over 43,000 panels have

been made for the AIDS Memorial Quilt

to remember people who were

    mothers or fathers . . .

    sons or daughters . . .

    brothers or sisters . . .

    aunts, uncles, or cousins . . .

    grandmothers, grandfathers, or grandchildren . . .

    husbands, wives, partners, or friends.

Each was part of the human family

that connects us all.

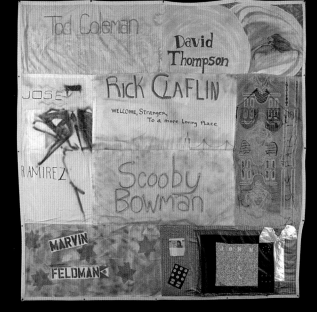

Author's Note

Making a panel for the NAMES Project AIDS Memorial Quilt is one way that people can remember someone who has died from the disease called AIDS. Following the tradition of quilting bees, most panels are made by a gathering of loving friends and family. The 3-by-6-foot panels are sewn with colors and images that remind the quilt makers of the person who died. Teddy bears, medals, heart-shaped buttons, and snapshots are just some of what's been sewn on. The panels are sent to San Francisco where volunteers stitch them together to make one enormous, colorful quilt.

The quilt was begun in 1987, and now has over 43,000 panels from all over the world. It has grown too large to be displayed in just one place, but parts of the quilt are sent around the country to be seen in schools, museums, synagogues, and churches.

If you would like to make a panel or to learn more about the NAMES Project, please write:

The NAMES Project AIDS Memorial Quilt

310 Townsend Street

San Francisco, CA 94107

Or see their Web site: http://www.aidsquilt.org